To Max

with my very best wishes

Lihas

The Eagle

Lilias Michael

authorHOUSE®

AuthorHouse™ UK Ltd.
500 Avebury Boulevard
Central Milton Keynes, MK9 2BE
www.authorhouse.co.uk
Phone: 08001974150

First published by AuthorHouse 8/22/2007

ISBN: 978-1-4343-2977-6 (sc)

Printed in the United States of America
Bloomington, Indiana

This book is printed on acid-free paper.

CHAPTER 1

The boy and his uncle approached the edge of the forest warily. Their bare feet made no sound and scarcely a footprint on the sparse grassed plain they had travelled over from their village some distance behind.

'Now Chato, have your spear at the ready. We must go further in to find an animal that is worthy to be your first kill. Don't hope for a bear but a cougar or elk would do. And if you miss first time then use your bow and arrow as fast as you can before the brute escapes.'

Chato nodded. Did Old Red Cloud have to remind him what he had to do? Such a fuss-pot, when he had been preparing for this hunting trip for quite some time. He was now fifteen and had to prove his manhood by killing a wild animal, the bigger the better. His family expected it and had sent him to live with his uncle who had been given the task of training him. He'd been shown how to make his own spear from a long straight branch of cedar wood and to fashion the head from stone which he whittled down to a thin sharp point. He had tied this as tightly as possible to the end of the shaft by long strips of thin leather from animal skins, hung up to dry until they were withered. His bow and arrows were his pride and joy and he cared for them as a mother cares for her child; keeping the shafts dry and storing them properly. The third weapon Red Cloud had taught him to make was a throwing stick or dart, particularly useful when an animal was close to hand. He carried all these weapons now; the bow and quiver slung over his shoulders, the dart firmly tucked into the belt of plaited hessian strands and the trusty spear in one hand. In his mind he was ready, and man enough to kill whatever came in their path. He told himself he was larger and braver than any of the other boys back in the village and now that the day had come he'd show them all what he could do with his weapons. He would catch the biggest, fiercest animal in the forest and return to the village triumphant.

His bare chest swelled as he took deep breaths before he and Red Cloud entered the dark green home of cedars, spruces, standing tall. Their eyes darted this way and that, steps slow, deliberate, each holding his spear high by one sinewy arm. Red Cloud may have had the title of 'Old' but his past hunting skills were for ever talked about in the tribe and he still enjoyed a chase.

There was a stillness around them except for the quiet chirping of small birds and the occasional chattering of squirrels; then a movement in the low foliage between the trees. Red Cloud grabbed Chato's free arm and put his fingers to his lips in a warning to stay quiet. They stood as if frozen. Then the boy relaxed.

'It's only a wolf,' he whispered. 'I want something bigger than that!'

'Hold your tongue!' the old man said in a low, slightly husky voice. 'Patience will bring its reward, but if you are too much in a hurry, the only thing you'll show for your arrogance *will* be a measly wolf or squirrel. Now be quiet and wait!'

Chato sniffed contempt at his uncle's words but remained silent and the two continued to creep forward.

Nothing further happened for some time, then suddenly there was a commotion, a frenzied mixture of sounds from birds as they rose from their perches in the trees; wolf and coyote howls, and the terrified screeching of small animals who darted from the undergrowth in panic. Once again Red Cloud stopped Chato in his tracks. His experience warned him that there must be something big ahead. They stood motionless and after a while saw a large brown bear, a grizzly, emerging from behind a tree some distance away. It was massive, its large head sitting atop humped shoulders. The pale brown, almost silvery fur shimmered in the shafts of sunshine finding their way through the foliage. It stopped and sniffed the air, head turning this way and that as a new smell invaded its nostrils. Chato's excitement grew. This was the one. This would be his trophy to take back to the village. Gauging the distance, he lifted his spear and before Old Red Cloud could stop him had thrown it towards the bear with all his might. The long shaft gave a whistling sound as it soared towards its prey but the stone point struck the bear's shoulder, glanced off and fell to the mossy ground. The bear gave a roar which made the air tremble and silenced the birds and the other animals for a fraction of time before they all, in frightened chorus, took up their concert once again. Chato, remembering Red Cloud's words, took the bow from his shoulder, but before he had pulled an arrow from its quiver, his uncle grabbed him by the waist, turned him around, pushing him forward and shouting,

'Run, boy, run! You've made him angry and he'll come after us. We must get out into the open.'

As if on winged feet they sped back to the forest entrance and into the open plain. The bear after its first howl of surprise and pain began its lumbering gait in pursuit. But the two had the advantage of running skills honed in childhood, and even Red Cloud's ability to race over the ground had scarcely left him in his advancing years. Chato's heart thumped in his chest, but the adrenalin racing through him conquered any fear and all he could think about was how to kill this bear, his trophy. He could still use his arrows and on an impulse, pulling one out and threading it into the bow he turned round and took aim. With a curse, Red Cloud nudged Chato's arm; the bow pointed upwards just as the arrow was released and flew high in the air to find its mark in the belly of an eagle that had been descending to discover what all the commotion was about. For one second it hung motionless then fell to the ground. At the same time Red Cloud turned to confront the bear which was rapidly approaching them and about to rise up on its hind legs to kill this enemy. With almost super-human strength Red Cloud threw his spear. The stone point embedded itself in the hairy chest, straight to the heart, and the beast fell at the old man's feet. It lay there, the eyes looking up at its killer in disbelief. Then they closed forever. The huge body gave a mighty twitch before it finally lay still.

Man and boy looked at their kills, one annoyed at what his uncle had done, the other so full of anger it was some time before he could burst out,

'Chato, you stupid, arrogant boy. You never listen to a thing I say. Do you see what you've done? Killed an eagle, the one bird that is sacred to our tribe, and I've had to kill the bear before it could attack us. This is no way for a brave hunter to act and your family are going to be so disappointed in you.' He shook his head and for a moment tears came to his eyes. After all it was he who had been given the task of training Chato. But his protégé, although standing with bowed head, had no feelings of remorse. No, he wanted to go on until he could prove he was a man.

'Uncle, there's still time for us to find another prey. Let's go back into the forest.'

'No!' roared Red Cloud. 'Enough of this vanity. We'll return to the village, taking the bear with us and I, to save your family and you the disgrace of your stupidity, shall tell how *you* killed it. But nothing will be said of the eagle, is that clear? Everyone would say that killing the sacred bird would bring bad luck to us all, so it's best that they are all ignorant of your infamy. But remember, I alone know what you've done and I'll never forget. I'll keep watching you and one of these days I'll think of some kind of punishment, believe me!'

Chato said nothing. What was there to say? His uncle would keep quiet to save his own face as well as his. *He* was still going home with a prized trophy, and now he'd earned his place amongst the men and the braves. His uncle's opinion of him didn't matter. It was the faces of his friends he wished to see when the bear's body was dragged into the compound. And so they each took hold of a leg of the beast and slowly dragging it along, made their way back to the village.

Behind them, left lying on the ground, abandoned, was the body of the bird, its once proud head lying awkwardly from a neck broken in its fall. The tawny feathers were now saturated with blood and the wings were crossed over as if trying to hide this disgrace. Suddenly, out of the sky soared three eagles, flying towards their fallen comrade. They swooped down, hovering over the body; then dropped to the ground. Their beady eyes inspected the carcase and slowly, by their claws, they lifted it by the head and the two wings. They carried it upwards and flew off over the forest, high above the trees. Down below there was nothing left of the chase that had ended so shamefully.

CHAPTER 2

B y the time Chato and Red Cloud arrived home the sun was low in the west and most of the braves had returned from their hunting. They entered the compound through the only gap in the poled fence which surrounded the village of several hundred wigwams. This gate of sorts consisted of two tall poles of cedar, hammered into the ground and held together at the top by a similar pole stretching from one to the other and resting on deep grooves. From this hung long ropes made from the hides of bison to which were attached small discs of copper. These moved in the breezes, making tinkling sounds and would also warn the inhabitants of any danger from the many wild animals which might, either by hunger or curiosity decide to pay them a visit during the dark of night.

In the centre of the compound was the biggest wigwam and outside, a little distance away stood a tall totem pole decorated with beautiful carvings of fish, birds and all sizes of animals. At the very top, so high that most people had to put their heads back to see it properly, was a carved eagle, painted in blues, purples, greens and with a huge yellow hooked beak. The eyes were set in either side of the head so that it appeared to be watching over everyone in the area. This was the house of the tribal head man, Eagle Eyes. He was sitting outside, cross-legged, observing each brave as he passed and taking note of the spoils of the day. Around the waists of many of them hung salmon and smelt from the broad river that passed by the village on the north side, snaking its way westwards; several men dragged a huge bison wrapped loosely in a blanket, its legs tied together with leather thongs. Wolves, deer, hung by the legs from stout branches and were being carried on the broad shoulders of the strongest. The old Chief seemed satisfied and smiled, showing black, broken teeth. His people would feed well tonight. He stood up and was about to enter his tent to give instructions to his woman to prepare a fire to cook the evening meal when Chato and Red Cloud came towards him, bent over and sweating with their labours of dragging the bear carcase across the plain. The old chief stared.

'Is that you, Red Cloud?'

Red Cloud nodded and breathlessly muttered 'yes.'

'Come here and tell me what you've been doing. And is that young Chato you have with you?'

The other man waited a little until his breathing became steadier then answered.

'Yes, Chief Eagle Eyes, my nephew. His family put him in my charge to be trained for manhood and he's been living with me. Today was the big test and we've been in the forest looking for a worthy kill.

And just look at what he has caught! This was an ugly creature, I can tell you, but Chato threw his spear so expertly that it caught the brute straight in the heart. He is surely a man now.'

At these last words Red Cloud's voice could not conceal a certain disdain and the old Chief, his long white hair blowing in the breeze that was beginning to swirl about the compound, looked straight into the other man's eyes. They had known each other for a long time and had held many discussions at the tribal powwows over the years. As their eyes locked he noticed a slight lowering of Red Cloud's eyelids and a reddening of his cheeks. He shifted his gaze to Chato who was looking at the ground, but with a proud arrogant look on his face. There was a mystery here, the old man thought. But this was not the time or the place to discover it. Instead he said,

'Congratulations, young lad. You have certainly proved your manhood. Now, once you've taken this bear to be skinned go to your parents to tell them the good news. There will be a coming-out ceremony to celebrate your bravery in a few days. Come to me here, Red Cloud, when you are finished. I want to know all about your hunt.'

He lifted his hand in salute, turned away and entered the wigwam behind him.

Once again Red Cloud and Chato lifted the bear's legs and dragged the body across the compound to an area where there was much activity in the skinning and gutting of the animals and fish that had been caught that day. The men did the heavy work of removing the pelts while the women, sitting crossed-legged on the hard earth, stripped the bones of flesh, gutted the fish and prepared everything for each family to collect and cook. When they saw the bear, and how big it was, there were cries of delight.

'Now that's what I call a bear,' said one woman, her hands deep inside the open belly of a young deer. 'Once the men have stripped it we'll butcher the remains, smoke them over the fire and hang them up. We'll need the meat when winter arrives. Any chance of your catching another like it soon, Chato?' This question was asked half-jokingly as she looked at Chato's still youthful frame. Red Cloud said nothing, his face inscrutable. Chato had the grace to blush a little, but answered,

'I'll do my best.'

The two men turned and went their separate ways. As the boy approached his parent's wigwam he squared his shoulders. Already he was putting out of his mind the fact that it had been the old man who finally killed the bear. All he could think about was how everyone, especially the other boys would be so envious. A few had passed their test in recent weeks, but none had caught such a large animal. They would have to give him respect now. Oh, it was going to be great to see their faces!

Red Cloud made his way to the Chief's tent. The flaps were open wide indicating that visitors could walk in unannounced. He bent his head and entered. Eagle Eyes sat at the far end, on a bear skin, his woman, silver-haired too, busying herself around a fire that was just beginning to flame. He motioned Red Cloud to draw near and said,

'Now tell me the truth of this matter. From your voice and the look on your face I have the feeling that all is not what you say it to be. Did that youth really kill that bear?'

The other man hesitated before answering. This was not what he'd expected. He'd been quite willing to support the lie to save Chato's face, but keeping the truth from his Chief---that was different.

'No, he did not. He bungled it and I had to save us both by killing the beast. I knew how devastated and disappointed his parents would feel if he came home disgraced, so I decided to tell the lie. I should have known, great Chief that nothing escapes your eyes!'

'At the moment this stupid boy is no doubt boasting to all his friends how brave he is. Should we expose him? If we do he'll never be able to hold his place amongst the tribe again.'

'There is some courage in him, I know there is,' said Red Cloud. 'But he needs to be brought to his senses. Leave it to me, Chief. I'm sure I can think up some scheme that will show him the true way to manhood. When I do I'll come to you for your approval.'

Eagle Eyes nodded and with a gesture indicated that the powwow was over. As Red Cloud went through the open flap of the wigwam he noticed that the sun had already set and the sky was a steadily darkening blue. He looked at the totem pole, at the eagle sitting on top and stopped in his tracks. Was it his imagination, or did the head bend towards him? Did the two black eyes come together, open wide and stare straight at him? He shivered, remembering the broken body of the bird left at the scene of Chato's stupidity. It was a bad omen, and for the sake of the tribe he had tokeep this knowledge to himself. But a part of him believed that the die was cast. Nothing but trouble would result in the boy's impetuosity (and his too, he had to admit.) Could something be done to avert a disaster? He was the only one to do it without revealing his motives. There and then he decided to think up a scheme that would save the tribe from dishonour and perhaps a terrible vengeance. Meanwhile   he must return to his own wigwam and greet Chato as if the deceit was of no importance. It was not going to be easy living a lie.

CHAPTER 3

Chato's pride and boastfulness know no bounds. Once his parents, sisters and brother had lavished praise upon him he went in search of his friends; the young braves and   girls he had known since childhood. His especial chum was Eskadi, a year older, who had passed his man-hood test already by bagging a huge elk. Its antlers were now displayed outside the family wigwam, tied to a small totem pole specially made by the boy's father and painted by his mother and sister. Chato was determined to go even further by having his bear's skin and fur stripped in one whole piece, and he had given instructions for this to be done in such an arrogant and boastful way that the men doing the stripping had laughed at him.

'So you think you're a man now, Chato, bringing back a bear?' said one.

'More like beginner's luck!' said another. 'Let's see what you can do tomorrow and the days after. It takes more than one kill to make a brave.'

They turned away from him and had continued with their work. Chato felt rebuffed, but had kept pressing them to do what he asked until finally they agreed. He wanted to bring the bear almost to life again by stuffing it with old blankets, wood shavings and anything he could lay his hands on. Then it would stand before his family tent, informing everyone who gazed at it that this was where the bravest boy in the village lived. Oh, yes he could just imagine how awe-struck they'd all be and maybe he'd stand beside it, telling and re-telling the tale of how he'd killed it.

He found Eskadi with a group of lads. A few giggling girls stood behind them. It was one of the younger boys who said, as Chato came up to them,

'Did you really kill a bear, Chato? I won't believe it until I see the body!'

'Of course I did, and it's over there waiting to be skinned. Old Red Cloud was with me but I was the one to spear it through the heart. Ask him if you like.'

Not a muscle of his face moved as this lie was spoken. Chato had persuaded himself of his own bravery so his part in the killing must be true. The young lads seemed duly impressed and the girls approached him, their eyes wide with admiration and begging him to tell them how he had done it. There was only one girl who mattered to him and that was Natane, twin sister of Eskadi. She was tall for a female, her features so beautifully sculptured and her long ebony black hair swept back in a plait to show small delicate ears. Chato could not help but love her; as did most of his friends. But he seemed to sense that she looked on him with a degree of favour and now as he recounted the meeting then the killing of the bear it was to her that he directed his words. He so wanted to be important in her eyes and as the tale unfolded he embellished it with more and more fantasies. Natane gazed at him in admiration. Her childhood friend was certainly a man now. Would he make a good spouse? Her parents, she knew, were already thinking of a marriage for her. Perhaps, now that Chato had proved himself, they would consider him. She drew nearer and sat down at his feet, drinking in every word.

They were all so engrossed that they did not notice Red Cloud passing by. But he heard the boasting, and stopped in his tracks. His first thought was to break in and condemn Chato for the liar he was. Then he realised this was not the time or place. He'd promised Chief Eagle Eyes to think up some scheme to punish Chato for his arrogance and dishonesty and this he must do. So he passed on. His own woman would shortly be preparing a meal for him and Chato. Suddenly he felt very hungry. It had been a long day.

By this time it had grown dark and the moon gazed down. He looked up at it. A full moon had always appeared kindly and comforting to him but was it so tonight? The vague patterns seemed darker, ominous as if giving a warning. He gave himself a shake as if to ward off evil spirits and continued on his way. But suddenly he was aware of a fluttering sound which gradually became louder and looking up he saw a large shadow slowly cover the moon until its brilliance vanished.

Then it gradually came to light again as the shadow moved on and to Red Cloud's horror it descended towards the village. The nearer it came the more menacing it appeared and Red Cloud suddenly realised that it wasn't a shadow. Birds! Hundreds of them. They hovered over the wigwams, screeching and chattering. Hawks, falcons, crows. But mostly eagles. The noise was so loud that whole families rushed out to find where it was coming from. The birds began to dive and swoop, each one targeting a brave, a woman, a child. They fastened their talons to heads and shoulders, pecked at hair and scalp, producing human screeching to mingle with their throaty sounds. For a time there was chaos, everyone running around in all directions. Some of the older braves fired arrows into the air and a few birds fell to the ground but this caused only more anguished wailing from some of the older inhabitants

'Oh, we are cursed!'

The noise and confusion overtook this peaceful community for some time until, as if at a signal, the cloud of birds turned, rising into the sky and quickly disappeared. The crying of the children, the moans from the injured continued but after a while there was silence, more dreadful than the noise itself. Then voices.

'What was that?' 'Where did these birds come from?' 'Why are they attacking us? Has someone offended them?'

No one could give an answer. Only Red Cloud, who had witnessed it all in horror, knew what had happened.

'It's the eagle's revenge,' he said to himself. This visit of the birds was meant as a warning. And it was really his fault. Chato had been disobedient, certainly, but perhaps he had been too hasty in taking him out on his first hunt. And he, Red cloud had been the one to deflect the arrow which killed one of the tribe's sacred birds and now bad luck and misery would come to all of them. Tears of frustration came to his eyes. Oh, that he had never agreed to take on the task of training his nephew. Family loyalty was one thing, but putting the whole tribe in danger could not be ignored. Now he knew he could no longer keep the truth to himself, even though he had given his word to the Chief. But how and when? Another meeting with Eagle Eyes would have to be arranged.

After a while, when emotions calmed down, the people returned to their tents, attending to the injured and still pondering over the strange visit of the birds. Red Cloud entered his wigwam where his woman had prepared the evening meal. Chato arrived shortly afterwards and they both sat down to eat, one with a defiant look on his face, the other solemn and sad. One eagle killed and the whole tribe to suffer.

'But it's not the tribe that is to blame. It's Chato who has brought dishonour upon us.' As he thought these words an idea began to grow. What if Chato was sent away? The birds wouldn't attack the village if he wasn't there. He had told the Chief that in his opinion the lad had courage, but lacked a degree of sense. So what if he was sent off down river to fend for himself; prove to everyone, once and for all that he was a real man. And if he didn't return, his death would be put down to martyrdom. The idea grew more and more attractive to Red Cloud and he smiled broadly. This brought a response from Chato who rather belligerently muttered,

'I don't know why you smile, Uncle. That was a very frightening experience back there. The people were terrified.'

'They had a right to be so. I told you that killing the eagle would bring dishonour to our tribe. What we saw was only the beginning. I also said back in the forest that I know the truth of your deceit and will find a way of punishing you. What that punishment will be I'll keep a secret until the very last day. Meanwhile I suggest you stop your stupid boasting and get on with the tasks your father will expect you to do now that you're a man!'

He stood up and took a long stone pipe from beside his blanket. Picking a few tobacco leaves from a pouch at his waist he crumbled them between his fingers and pushed them down into the bowl. Then he took a long thin taper of wood shavings, lit it from the fire and put the lit end into the tobacco, inhaling deeply. He gave a harsh cough then exhaled smoke before going to the flap of the tepee, opening it and stepping out into the deep night. He slowly walked up and down, smoking quietly, enjoying the flavour and taste of the native plant. He always thought deeper and clearer with the pipe in his mouth and now these thoughts were formulating a plan to rid the tribe of the bad luck the eagle's death was about to bring them.

CHAPTER 4

The next day an atmosphere of fear lay like a blanket over the homes of the families. There were no children playing outside, no laughter or shouts of youthful happiness. Their parents feared a return of the birds and were keeping them inside the tents, much to the disgust of some boys who would have liked the opportunity to fire off a few arrows. But this was absolutely forbidden. Mothers and fathers had to recite over and over why no one should shoot down an eagle.

'They are sacred to our culture. This is their territory and we are only permitted to live on this land provided we respect them and never, *ever,* kill them for food or for any other reason. They must be angry for them to attack us like this, but why?'

No one could give an answer to the question that was on everyone's lips. Only Chato, and he was saying nothing. His parents' pride in his achievement overtook any idea that there might be a connection between the hunting test and the attack of the birds. It must be somebody else who had angered them.

For the older braves the day's work went on as usual. Hungry mouths had to be fed, and once the sun appeared over the mountains, they set off, bows and quivers slung over their shoulders, spears held tightly in their hands, ready to be thrown at the first sign of a decent trophy. Some were more adept at spearing fish and they made their way to the river behind the village which began as a stream from the mountain rocks to the east and was now broad but still fordable at certain spots. Sure-footed in their strong bare feet they stepped across on the large stones and boulders which they had placed themselves earlier that season; backwards and forwards, gazing into the shallow waters, looking for the salmon which were in plenty at that time. At first they could see nothing. Then,

'Look. Look!' shouted one brave. 'There they are.' He paused. ' But they're dead!'

His companions followed his gaze and sure enough, large salmon and small smelt were floating on the surface of the waters, side up and with one wide-opened eye looking blindly at them. There was nothing alive for them to spear. Why was this? What had killed them?

The braves jumped into the water, desperately searching for a catch. Several of them speared the fish that lazily floated round their ankles but when they pulled them up there wasn't a flicker of life. The men splashed about, some of them getting into deeper water, but not a single live fish could they see. The leader of the group, one of Chief Eagle Eyes' sons, finally said,

'It's no use. Something terrible has happened. Let's get back to the bank and go further down river. There might be live fish there.'

But there weren't. As the waters became deeper, more and more bloated, dead fish rose to the surface. The braves had never experienced such a thing. What would the women say when they returned with not a single fish for their labours? They looked to the Chief's son, Dyami for guidance. He shook his head.

'There's nothing to be done. We must go back and inform my father who will send a smoke signal to the tribe further up river for help. I shall take one fish for him to see. We can only hope that tomorrow the fish will be plentiful again.'

He grabbed a large salmon that was brushing against his legs, pushed a finger through its gaping mouth to make a hole, threaded a short length of thin leather through the hole and tied it to a leather belt round his waist. Dejectedly, they all waded back to the shore and began the journey home. Their early return was unexpected and unwelcome to the women who were used to their own company for most of the day. They approached Chief Eagle Eyes' wigwam where he and Red Cloud had been discussing Chato and whether to tell the people of his lying and cheating. Before they had decided on punishment they heard the men passing by and came out to meet them. The Chief saw his son and immediately called,

'Dyami, why are you home so early? Has something happened?'

The brave approached him.

'Father, the fish in the river have died. We searched and searched but not a live one could we find. I've brought one for you to see.'

The Chief and Red Cloud wrinkled their noses at the smell of this rotting fish. They looked at one another. During their powwow they had spoken about the evils that might befall the village because of Chato's stupidity. Now it seemed they were right to be worried. However,

'It might just be a sickness. You can all try again tomorrow. Meanwhile, the other braves will be returning with their game later today so we'll have enough meat for tonight. Now go and explain to your women what has happened, but on no account mention disease or bad luck. We don't want a panic.'

Each man went his separate way, not relishing the tale he had to tell to an angry woman and a hungry family.

Red Cloud with a worried look on his face, said,

'Is this the beginning, Chief?'

Eagle Eyes was about to reply when through the village gate trooped the rest of the hunters. They marched up to the Chief, holding out empty hands.

'Finished already? Where are your catches?' asked their Chief.

There was a long silence, no man wishing to admit their disgrace of coming home with nothing. Eagle Eyes pointed at another of his sons.

'Patamon. Surely you can tell us.'

Patamon reddened and then, stuttering the words, said,

'My Father, we couldn't find a single beast in the forest. Not even a wolf! There were no sounds to indicate their presence and we just waited and waited. There was a strange light that we had never seen before, eerie and a bit frightening. Some of the men ran in much farther than they had ever gone and when they returned they insisted we all get back to our homes quickly. They said they had seen evil spirits floating amongst the trees and couldn't run away quick enough.'

The Chief took in this news with a heavy heart, but tried not to show his son how worried he was.

'Scared were you? And you call yourselves braves? Huh! A lot of girls you are! How are we all to eat tonight? No fish, no meat and very little corn. The flesh of the bear caught yesterday has not been hung long enough to be eaten, so it's going to be squashes and pumpkins with some berries to put into our mouths. And that's no food for braves! You'd better make sure that tomorrow will bring more success. Now off with you all, and I hope you can find decent excuses else the women will give you a bad time, that's for certain.'

With bowed heads and looking extremely dejected, the men went their separate ways.

Red Cloud who had listened to this with more and more apprehension, turned to the Chief, and in a low voice said,

'It's beginning. If something isn't done soon our people will slowly starve. Give me permission to send Chato away to fend for himself. It's our only chance. Surely if he has left these parts, the eagle might follow him and leave us alone.'

The old Chief thought for a moment. It seemed a drastic step to take, but it might work.

'Very well, Red Cloud, that's what we'll do. However our people must be told. If they are to be the sufferers then they have the right to know who it was that made the eagles so angry. Send out as many messengers as you can to inform everyone that there will be a council meeting immediately and that Chato will be put before them to admit his guilt and his lying.'

The other man put his hands on both sides of his head, and stayed like this for some time. He felt shame for his family and shame for himself. But feelings and emotions were not the issue here. The tribe had to be saved at all costs and if that meant banishing his nephew, then so be-it.

'My best plan, I think, is to send him off in a canoe, down river. I'll give him some supplies but he'll have to hunt for the bulk of his food. He says he is a man. Well now he'll be given the chance to prove it. He's so full of his own importance I doubt he'll come back with his tail between his legs! In the end of the day it might even make a true brave of him.'

Eagle Eyes gave a laugh.

'You're a wily old fox, Red Cloud. Yes, that is the best thing for him and we can only hope his absence will remove the terror that's slowly engulfing our village.'

'We shall see,' answered Red Cloud, and with a slight bow and a hand to his heart, he turned away to spread the word that there was to be a tribal meeting outside the Chief's wigwam as soon as possible. This information did not go down well with some families as the women were trying desperately to produce meals from almost nothing and there was a great deal of mumbling and grumbling. But slowly they emerged from their wigwams, the women with sleepy papooses strapped to their backs, the older children wide-eyed, wondering, the braves strong, upright, and curious to hear what the tribe councillors would have to say. Gradually they all gathered outside the Chief's tent, the tall totem pole in their midst with the eagle at the top whose large black eyes gleamed menacingly

CHAPTER 5

Chato was sitting in Red Cloud's wigwam, awaiting the meal that his aunt was preparing and grumbling underneath her breath at how little there was to cook. He had seen the braves returning earlier and knew that something dreadful was happening. For one thing they shouldn't have come home until sunset and they were empty handed. No fish, no meat; how could that be? The river was always teeming with fish at this time of year, and he knew, from his hunting trip the previous day that the forest was full of game; birds and animals.

His uncle and aunt had forbidden him to leave the tent for fear of the birds returning and this made him petulant and angry.

'I'm not a child any more. I've proved myself a brave and can look after myself.'

'Look after yourself?' said Red Cloud. 'You haven't proved anything to me yet. You're still full of your mother's milk. It'll take more than one hunting trip to put some muscle on you. So, for your family's sake at least, you will do as we demand.'

He said not another word and had left the tent to go and meet with Chief Eagle Eyes, leaving an embittered and scowling Chato at the mercy of his aunt who had a long history of knowing how to deal with wayward boys. And so he had sat at the open flaps of the tent, whittling at a willow branch with a stone flint and dreaming of his bear skin which at that moment was hanging in its entirety from the bough of a juniper tree, its inside scoured to make it dry quicker. Once it was ready he'd collect it, stuff it and then place it outside his family's wigwam. Not Red Cloud's. He was his parent's son and only they should have the honour of displaying it to all the tribe. Oh, they would be so proud!

Normally at this time there would be an aroma of meat roasting over the open fire, the smoke finding its way upwards and through a narrow hole at the top of the conical tent. But all the food Mahala, his aunt, was cooking seemed to be corn cakes roasted in sunflower oil, beans and some meagre flesh from captured pigeons. No life-giving deer or bison meat fit for braves. Chato wrinkled his brow in disgust.

'Is that all we're to eat?' he asked. 'Didn't you save anything from yesterday's hunt?'

'Shut your mouth. You wouldn't speak to me in that fashion if my man was here. The braves brought back nothing today, so nobody has sufficient food for their bellies tonight. Why that is, I-----'

She broke off as Red Cloud entered, having heard the conversation. Without commenting on the rudeness of his nephew he said in an authoritative voice,

'Chief Eagle Eyes is holding a council meeting around the totem pole *now*. The people are there already and you and I are late. So get up from your hindquarters and come with me. You, woman, come too. And don't worry about the meal!'

He pushed both of them through the flaps, hurrying them along to join the gathered crowd, Mahala protesting that her food would be ruined. Red Cloud led them through the restless, but curious tribespeople until they were standing in front of the Chief's tent. He, as yet had not appeared and there was a low mumbling that was becoming gradually louder as he kept them waiting. Chato could see his parents with their other children and tried to catch their attention but they were too busy discussing the situation with their neighbours to notice him. He guessed the council meeting had something to do with the attack of the birds, and suddenly he felt fear. Had his shooting down of the eagle really been the reason for the terror they had brought to the village? But only Red Cloud knew about it. And anyway it had been the old man who grabbed his arm and the arrow struck the eagle instead of the bear. So by rights the bear *ought* to have been his catch and it was not his fault that he had killed an eagle. These reassurances calmed him down before the flaps of Eagle Eyes' wigwam opened and the Chief himself stepped out.

There was an immediate hush, all eyes turning towards him. He was an impressive sight, tall, his thick silver hair hanging beyond the shoulders and with a narrow band of twisted grasses tied round his forehead, a long eagle feather jutting up at the back. His face was painted in blue stripes from chin to forehead, giving him a ferocious look. He had covered his bare chest with a sleeveless over-shirt made from buffalo skin and reaching to his knees. Below these were thick fur leggings and his feet were covered in soft doe skin leather. He held a long staff of cedar wood in his hand which, like the totem pole sported an eagle at the top, and he looked round the assembled people with a fierce, angry glare in his black eyes. There came an 'Ahhhhhh' from the crowd which was silenced by Eagle Eyes raising the staff and pointing it towards them. He then looked at Red Cloud and Chato.

'Approach!'

They stepped forward.

The Chief raised his head and spoke to the assembly.

'I have ordered this council, to bring to the notice of all that we have a liar and a cheat in our village. The reason why we have no food today and that we have been attacked by the birds is because this boy here,' pointing to Chato, 'has killed one of our sacred birds. He has returned from his first hunting, giving the lie that he killed a bear when in fact it was Old Red Cloud who did it.'

There were gasps from the crowd and Chato's father shouted out, 'No, no, that can't be!'

'Yes, and his uncle will give you proof. Come and speak to them, my friend.'

Red Cloud, his face sad as he turned to the startled tribe, and his voice wavering, gave them an account of all that had happened the previous day. From the boy's stupidity at trying to kill the bear and how the eagle had been struck by the arrow when he, Red Cloud had prevented Chato from aiming at the bear again.

'That bear was very, very angry and it was only with all my strength that I killed it before it killed us.'

'But why did you not tell us the truth?' shouted Chato's father.

'It was loyalty to our family and I didn't want the tribe to be alarmed at the killing of an eagle. But I can see now how wrong I was. Chato has shown that he is unworthy to be a brave.'

There was a low murmur which steadily grew to a roar like thunder as the people heard this. The women encircled their children with strong arms as if to ward off evil spirits; papooses began to wail as the unaccustomed noise blasted their ears and the men raised their fists at Chato, some shouting,

'Kill him! Kill him!'

Chato, who had been standing as if turned to stone, looked back at them and what he saw in their faces terrified him. Strangely he had felt no fear when the bear was attacking, but this was something different. He looked over at his parents for comfort but there was none. His mother wept loudly and painfully, his father, usually so proud in his bearing, suddenly stooped as if he had aged in a moment of grief. The Chief held up a hand.

'No! Killing him is not the answer. The eagle's death was not a deliberate kill. It was all due to this boy's stupidity and arrogant pride. Red Cloud has explained that. Our immediate concern is to appease the birds and to bring an end to the terrible revenge they are bringing upon us. Red Cloud has a plan which might be the answer.'

The other man, who had ignored his nephew all this time, now turned to him and spoke loudly to the assembly.

'This boy, who so desperately wishes to be thought of as a strong brave, is still a   child. You know that in your heart, Chato. But I also know you have courage. Perhaps I pushed you too hard. Your first hunting was too soon and you've come to grief. However the tribe's welfare is more important than your pride so you are going to have the chance to redeem yourself and perhaps the eagle's revenge will cease. We shall give you a canoe, some provisions and set you off alone down river, dealing with every situation that comes along. Then you will learn what being a brave really means. You will travel through territory that even our Chief hasn't seen----and hopefully you'll return to us, more worthy of your place in our tribe.'

The crowd heard this in silence, some nodding in approval. Then when Red Cloud finished one by one the cries were taken up.

'Yes, send him away!'

'Let the birds follow HIM and leave us alone.'

'If he isn't here, they won't come back again and there will be fish in the river and meat in the forest again.'

One brave rushed towards Chato and would have knocked him to the ground but Eagle Eyes roared,

'Nooooo! There is no need to punish him by violence. Red Cloud knows what to do. This meet is now at an end, so all of you return to your homes and continue cooking   what food you have. Tomorrow, when everything is ready for Chato to leave, Red Cloud and I shall see him off then our braves can go hunting again. I suggest you give offerings to the Spirit of the Wind for their success.' He turned to Chato.

'Now, go to your parents. Stay with them this night, for they need to know if you are showing remorse. Red Cloud, I leave you to do what you have to do.'

Without another word he returned to his tent, closing the flaps behind him in an act of   dismissal. Muttering under their breath the people slowly left the compound, but occasionally looking back at Chato and shaking their fists. He stood, red-faced, fear gripping him. All his boastfulness returned to haunt him. He had seen the looks on the faces of his friends, especially Natane, as Red Cloud had spoken and knew he'd never be able to impress them again. And now he was being sent away. He gazed at Red Cloud.

'When shall I have to leave?' he asked.

'Tomorrow. I shall put together all that I think you need. And I'll give you my own canoe. It is strongly built for the hazards you might come across in your travels.'

The boy swallowed hard at these words. Already the unknown was looming large and frightful.

'Come to me at first light and I will tell you what you have to do. Also tell your   parents that you will require all the heavy clothing they can give you. The full sun season is coming to an end and the cold icy winds will begin to blow as you travel down river. Is that clear?'

Chato nodded and with a heavy heart made his way to his parents' wigwam to face their shame and then to spend a sleepless night, imagining all kinds of dangers and wild beasts that would lie ahead of him in what could have been a mighty adventure if it wasn't for the terrible disgrace of it all.

Chapter Six

As the sky began to lighten from its deep impenetrable blackness, Red Cloud rose from his bed of thin branches covered with deerskin, leaving behind Mahala, still sleeping and snoring gently. He looked at her. He thought of the children she'd borne, only to have them snatched from her early in infancy and now she was too old to give him a son. He'd imagined that by taking in Chato, still a boy, this would have filled the emptiness and allowed her maternal capabilities to come to the fore again. But it hadn't been successful. She'd taken an instant dislike to him which Chato sensed, resulting in his arrogant and rude behaviour towards her. There was always a tension when the three of them sat down to eat.

'She won't be sorry to see him go,' Red Cloud thought.

But oh, the shame of it! Chato was from his side of the family, not hers, so perhaps she'd never understand the sorrow, over and above the anger they all felt. The punishment was just, but that didn't make it any easier to accept. He gave a huge sigh and, opening the flaps of the wigwam, stepped out into the cool air of first light and breathed deeply. Would Chato be on time? Had his parents forgiven him and given their blessing for a safe journey? He had not long to wait for an answer. From out of the gloom, making his way between the wigwams, his nephew strode towards him. He wore doe skin leggings from ankles to above the knees, and a short apron-type leather skirt, front and back. His torso was bare and his face had been daubed in stripes and half-circles with a red vegetable dye. The long dank hair hung to his shoulders.

'His mother at least has forgiven him,' thought Red Cloud. 'She has painted the signs to ward off evil spirits as he travels. That is good.'

He noted that the boy carried his bow and quiver of arrows over his shoulder. One hand grasped a short spear while the other held a large wicker basket.

'You've come in good time, Chato. What provisions have you in that bag?'

His nephew opened it to reveal corn cakes, bean pods, several squash, blackberries and pieces of dried meat wrapped in rabbit skin. Folded up were a one-piece tunic, a fur cape with a hood, soft leather foot coverings and a blanket his mother had made from plant fibres.

'That seems enough to keep you going for several days. After that you'll hunt and fish for yourself. Are you up to it, Chato?'

The boy gulped, and answered hoarsely,

'I shall try to do as you all expect of me.' Then in a final show of bravado,

'I know I can do it!'

Red Cloud said merely, 'Hm. Well, we shall see.'

He looked at the spear Chato held in his hand.

'That's too short.'

He turned back into the wigwam and a short time later appeared with a long pole, its fierce-looking flint at the end honed to the sharpness of a needle.

'Here, take this. It has saved me many times. But remember, don't go looking for bears! Avoid them at all costs. Now let's go down to the river to my canoe.'

As the men walked towards the place that would be the beginning of Chato's enforced journey, he had time to reflect. So much had happened so quickly that he seemed to be in a state of shock. His mind couldn't yet grasp he'd done anything seriously wrong. He still believed that if it hadn't been for his uncle's interference, he'd have killed the bear and the eagle would have flown away. And now he was being sent off in disgrace. It was unfair. Anger rose within him. He'd show them; He *would* come back, with as many pelts as the canoe would carry, to prove that he *was* a brave, and as courageous as any of them in the village. His steps took on a more confident pace and Red Cloud smiled as he kept up, saying to himself,

'The boy is determined. It's not going to be easy, but perhaps, just perhaps, this might be the making of him.'

They reached the river and there, beached, was Red Cloud's canoe. It was magnificent. Years before, when he had been a young brave, he and his brothers cut down a red cedar tree. They'd split it down the middle and slowly, by burning and scraping, gouged out two boats. Red Cloud, being the elder had first choice and soon he made it his own by softening the inside with boiling water and shaping it to his special design. Ever after he'd cared for it as a mother cares for her child and his many fishing trips were successful only because his stout craft had manoeuvred the river hazards with ease.

'Do you really wish me to have your own canoe?' asked Chato, for he knew how proud his uncle was of it.

'Yes, I do. I'm becoming too old to go out on it anymore and your aunt wants me to stop. I fear you may come across many dangers and if you have a strong canoe to carry you, you'll feel safer. I've given you two paddles. Now let's get your things in and let me see you seated. There's a layer of bark and twigs for you to sit on.'

Chato leaned forward and gently laid the basket and his weapons in the foot of the canoe. The sun was beginning to shed its early rays over the river and it lit up the interior of the boat. The boy let his hand run over the sides and marvelled at the smoothness. This had been built by a craftsman. He was just about to climb in himself when he became aware that Red Cloud had turned away. Looking up, he saw Chief Eagle Eyes approaching, two of his sons behind him, the same two who had led the disastrous hunt the previous day.

'Everything ready, Red Cloud? And you, Chato, have you all that you need?'

Chato nodded but could see the young braves looking at him sneeringly. He tried not to show he was affected but tears came quickly to his eyes. Turning his head he blinked them away and pushed out his chin in an effort to give the impression that he didn't care. Red Cloud took him by the arm, saying,

'My nephew is just about to leave, Chief. Get into the boat, Chato and we'll push you into the water.'

The boy climbed in, sat down and slowly the others pushed the canoe over the sand and shingles to the water's edge. It launched itself smoothly and lay on the surface, rocking slightly. The river flowed at this point away from the sun, and Chato picked up one of the paddles, guided the craft until it was pointing down stream, then waited. The men on the bank stood solemnly; Eagle Eyes raised his hands high above his head and chanted,

'Spirit of the Skies, look over this boy. Bring him to a state of wisdom and strength. We leave him in your hands.'

Chato began to paddle and the canoe moved slowly and silently along the smooth waters towards a destination as yet unknown, and through territory that would both delight and terrify him. As the rhythm of the paddles from one side to the other became steady Chato's spirits lifted and he suddenly began humming. Perhaps this enforced exile might not be so bad after all. He was being given another chance to prove he was a brave, and brave he was. Yes, he'd show them!

CHAPTER 7

As Chato paddled the canoe down river that morning, taking him farther and farther away from the village and home life, his mood was more confident. He felt strong and eager to take on this adventure. Regrets at leaving behind his parents and family had long left his mind. After all he had really become separated from them when he went to live with Red Cloud and in a sense had outgrown them. Or so he told himself.

'They don't know that I'm a man now,' he thought, as he passed the paddle from one side to the other, pushing the canoe forward. His elation grew with each stroke but then he became aware that it was becoming increasingly more difficult for the blades to cut through the water. On realising this he looked about and to his amazement there were dead fish around the canoe, floating on the surface. But how could this be? How could dead fish float *upstream* when the current was flowing in the opposite direction? He had no time to dwell on these questions as more and more of them crowded in on the craft. Frantically he pushed some aside with the paddle and tried to continue, but there were too many. They looked at him with their dead eyes and he recoiled in shock when a couple suddenly leapt out of the water, landing in the bottom of the canoe. Others followed until they were covering his feet and legs with their   bloated, stinking bodies. He gagged at the smell, but reached for his spear and with shouts of 'Take that and THAT,' he jabbed at this one and that one, throwing them out of the canoe. But as fast as he did this more fish would leap out of the water and land on top of the others. The canoe rocked from side to side as it became weighted down. Suddenly he was afraid. Was the adventure to end so quickly by his floundering in the river and losing all his precious supplies? Desperately he thought of the appeals he had heard his parents and even Red Cloud make when things had gone wrong for them; to the wind spirit, the river spirit, and even the sky spirit. Pulling the paddle into the canoe, he took a deep breath and as loud as he could, shouted,

'Oh Great Spirit of the River, help me. Remove these dead fish. Bring life back to the river and let me continue my journey in peace.'

In an instant, dark clouds covered the sun, high overhead; there was an angry clap of thunder and rain fell from the skies. A wind sprang up and the waters were whipped into a frenzy of waves, whirlpools till the canoe took on a life of its own, rising, dipping until Chato was sure it would overturn. As he grasped each side to keep steady, a voice suddenly spoke.

Chato, Chatooooo! The Spirit of the River hears you. But why should I answer you? You have killed a mighty hunter of

the air, brought shame on your tribe and your punishment is just. To redeem yourself you must make amends to the Great Eagles by showing your sorrow at their loss. Are you willing to do this?

Chato, his face growing pale, trembled as he heard these words. His confidence suddenly left him and he wished, oh, how much he wished that Red Cloud was there. The old man would know what to do. He understood the Spirits. There was a long silence, broken by,

Well--------?

'Oh yes,' cried Chato. 'I am so very sorry that my arrow killed the eagle. I did not mean to do it. But really it was my Uncle who nudged my arm and my aim went wild.'

It was your stupidity and arrogance that caused it all The dead fish shall disappear but you still have a long way to go before you can be looked upon as a brave. This has been the first of your trials. Make sure you go forward with more humility.

The wind, and the voice ceased and the dark clouds disappeared. The river became calm, serene and once more the sun shone down from a deep blue sky. To Chato's relief the canoe was empty of dead fish and was sitting on the water normally. He looked around. Had he been dreaming? Did the Spirit of the River really talk to him? But there were no dead fish, floating anywhere. Then some distance away he saw a salmon take a leap out of the water, then another. They were alive!

Quickly he grabbed the paddle, and manoeuvred the canoe forward once more. Yes, there were fish aplenty to catch whenever he wished.

Red Cloud's sturdy canoe handled well and after a while Chato put the conversation with the Spirit of the River out of his mind and began to enjoy the steady movement over the water. Only once did he look up when he heard the deep throated calls of birds. Two large bald eagles were hovering above him. One swooped down and landed on the front end of the craft, looking at him with beady eyes. Chato stared back but said nothing. He had made his apology; what more did they want? The other one circled over his head, wings outstretched, but made no attempt to drop down. Suddenly angry, Chato shouted at them.

'Go away! I'm not going to harm any of you.'

The first eagle croaked and Chato heard, *We'll get you!* Then they both flew up and away. Afterwards he was sure it had been his imagination that made him hear the words. His experience with the River Spirit was making him nervous and jumpy.

He continued paddling, but soon began to feel hungry. At this point the river was narrower than it had been when he first began his journey and turning the canoe he paddled towards a small shingled beach, beyond which were trees and bushes, then the ground rose to a forest of tall cedars and pines. He pushed the craft with all his might and it came out of the water with a rush, and embedded the prow into the sand and stones. He grabbed his weapons, the wicker basket, and jumped out, wading through the shallow waters until he felt the warmth of the pebbles on his bare firm feet. He ran towards the bushes and sat down. He gazed back at the river, so calm, peaceful and a surge of pride swept through him. He would succeed.

Opening the basket, he took out the food his mother had packed. The blackberries and nuts could be eaten as they were, but the dried meat had to be softened. That meant a fire. Quickly he gathered some small branches and piled them in a heap on the sand. Thank goodness his mother had remembered to give him a wooden bowl and his father, a renowned hunter himself, had put into the basket two pieces of flint. He rubbed these together over the twigs, and after a time smoke arose from a small flame. This he made larger by blowing gently and soon a fire was born. He nurtured this with more twigs and dried leaves and picking up some small stones he placed them over the flames. Then, taking the bowl down to the river's edge he filled it with water. He carried it back to be filled with the stones which, as soon as they became hot enough were picked out with his bare hands so quickly that he scarcely felt any pain. He did this several times until the water was bubbling and then dropped the dried meat into it. Slowly the pieces expanded into their original shapes; slices of liver, pigeon breast, deer rump. Chato's hunger increased as they gradually softened, cooked and sent out their appetizing aromas. He soon was enjoying a meal as satisfying as any Red Cloud's woman had produced. At least that is what he told himself as he sat back against the bush and gradually went to sleep.

The sleep lasted some time as his mind and body relaxed. When he woke the sun was lower in the sky. There was stillness. No sounds of birds or small animals.

'I must go on,' he thought. 'Before I settle for the night I have to catch some fish and game, but I'd rather travel farther.'

He gathered up the remainder of the berries and meat, hurriedly pushed them into the basket along with the flints. Grabbing his weapons he ran to the canoe, slid it back into the water and jumped in. He grabbed the paddle and feverishly sent the canoe on its journey down river once more. He kept looking this way and that for some sign of a wooded area where there would be animals small enough for him to kill and eat. Hunting the bigger animals would come later.

As he paddled he became aware that the river was broadening and descending into a ravine. There came a distant rumble. The noise became louder and he saw ahead that the water, so calm and gently flowing before, was churning, writhing as it tried to make its way through rocks and boulders. The canoe was glancing against these rocks which seemed to have appeared from nowhere and he was finding it increasingly difficult to control it. He paddled desperately but the craft had a mind of its own and the paddle was swept from his hands. He picked up the second one but it too went the same way. By this time he knew where he was. He had heard the braves talking of the 'angry waters.' How some of them had never returned. Panic-stricken he grabbed his spear, threw his bow and quiver of arrows over his shoulder and waited. The canoe raced on, as if unaware of its ultimate destiny, struck a large rock and turned over, throwing Chato into the hostile river. He went under, the spear was swept from his hand, and in surprise he gulped in a large mouthful of water. Using his legs, he pushed himself back to the surface, and spluttering, coughing, he managed to take in a breath before he submerged again. This happened a few times before he had the strength to swim to the canoe which was still turned turtle but now sandwiched between two rocks. The wicker basket was floating beside it, empty, with the contents bobbing up and down, but in danger of following the current downstream. Chato knew he would be unable to right the canoe just then, so the most important thing was to rescue his belongings. Making sure the bow and arrows were firmly over his shoulder, he swam towards the basket, then slowly, treading water, picked up as many items of clothing and tools he could reach. The heavy things such as the flints had sunk to the bottom, but there was nothing that could be done about that, he thought. He was just glad he was still alive and the most important thing was to get on to dry land. He looked towards the bank of the river and saw a small cove at the foot of a sheer cliff. It looked most inhospitable, but it was the only alternative to a watery grave. But how to reach it across the turbulent river? He cast his eyes around and saw that between himself and the bank there were rocks of various sizes, separated by foaming water. He swam to the nearest, and slowly, fighting his way from one to the other made his way to the cove, and fell down on the firm ground, exhausted. He was safe, but for how long?

CHAPTER 8

Chato lay, legs splayed out over the thin sand, half conscious. The picture of a young, energetic boy setting out on an enforced adventure had disappeared. His long blue-black hair was a tangle of twigs and sodden leaves, picked up as he desperately fought his way to the surface of the river. His body was scratched from contact with stones and rocks and all that was left of the clothes he'd worn were a few torn remnants, scarcely covering his nakedness. The bow and quiver of arrows had slipped down from his shoulder and now were loosely attached to his forearm. Night had fallen and a half moon barely illuminated the cove, so high were the cliffs on either side.

It was a desolate scene that greeted Chato as he eventually came to his full senses. He sat up slowly and looked around. He could just make out the river, still racing and roaring towards its climax but he was too far away to see the canoe. The basket lay some distance from him and disentangling his weapons he crawled towards it and examined the contents or what was left of them. He'd managed to salvage all the clothes, 'and the blanket, thank goodness,' he thought, but they were sodden. The food was gone, the flints too, but the greatest loss was his spear. Now all he had as weapons were the arrows. The tears came to his eyes and for a brief moment he was a child again. He longed for his mother's arms to comfort him as they had done not so very long ago. But there was no one here to help. Tears became sobs and the pent up feelings of pride, elation, then frustration that he had experienced these last few days escaped in gut-wrenching sounds that echoed round the cliffs above. The noise frightened him and he stopped, breathing deeply until his body was calm again. Was this he, Chato, behaving like a child? Braves didn't show tears or that they were afraid. He looked up at the dark sky and almost without thinking, shouted 'Help me, help me!' to any spirit that would hear him.

There was no sudden rushing of the wind, no whispering voice and at first he thought his plea had not been heard. Just as he was about to call out again, he realised that the river had ceased its savage thunderous noise, and peering through the gloom he saw that it was now flowing along quietly, by-passing the rocks and lapping against them gently. He could hardly believe this and getting to his feet he walked slowly towards the edge of the water. The stillness was in marked contrast to his fated journey earlier. Then he heard the fluttering of wings and suddenly there appeared a flock of birds, hovering over him; black crows, falcons, hawks, but mostly eagles. Where had they come from? Looking up he saw more of them perched on the cliff tops, like sentinels.

Two large eagles flew down and landed at his feet, wings outstretched. To his horror one of them spoke.

We know who you are, Chato. We saw you kill our brother. Our flock wanted you to be killed as revenge, but the General Council dissuaded us from this. Instead you are to be given the chance to redeem yourself by undertaking many tasks as you travel along this river and to show that you really are a brave of the bravest and to make amends for your crime. Are you willing to do this?

Chato wanted nothing more than to be free of these birds and without hesitating said,

'Oh, yes, yes! I've already made my apology to the Spirit of the River and I now make it to *you*,' extending his arm to include all the birds. 'I shall take on any task that comes before me for I have to prove myself to my family back at the village too.'

The eagle spoke no more, merely gazed at Chato with is large eyes. Seemingly satisfied with what he saw, he and his companion flew off, up over the cliffs, followed by the complete flock. Before they disappeared the spokesbird turned and in a low croaking voice that echoed between the rocks, gave out the word,

Remember!

Chato shivered. What was happening to him? Birds talking, winds whispering, in a language that he could understand. Once again he glanced at the quiet river trying to see if his canoe was still wedged between the rocks, but the light was poor and it was too far away. Then he saw something floating towards him. He waded out and grasped it. His spear! It was undamaged and with a great shout of joy he held it above his head. He searched around for the flints, dragging his feet over the pebbles below the shallow waters, but there was no sign of them. It seemed like a calamity, for how could he make fire? How was he to dry off the sodden clothing which he'd need soon in the evenings now that the sun season was ending? And what could he collect or hunt as food in this narrow place at the foot of the cliffs? Cliffs! Of course! Cliffs meant rocks so he would look around for flint rock. There must be some here, for all the families at the village used it to make fire and the braves always brought back supplies from their hunting trips. He walked towards the base of the nearest cliff and began, with hands and feet to search the loose stones that had fallen from the top. It took a little time for him to discover pieces of the hard grey rock that he knew would produce the spark to make fire. Gathering a handful he returned to where his basket and weapons lay and sat down, placing the spear carefully alongside.

But what to use to make flames? There were no bushes or trees around, only stones and sand. Then he thought of the blanket. It had been made by his mother from plant fibres and bark. Surely he could make fire from that. But it was still too wet. . Frustration swept over him. He'd have to wait until next sun for it to dry out, and he was so hungry. As if sensing his thoughts, a few birds, kestrels, kittiwakes, flew down from the cliff and hovered around him, twittering, then returned to their nesting places in the rocks.

'These cursed birds!' he cried out, as they came again, flying to and fro. Then suddenly he realised their meaning. Bird nests might mean eggs. But if they hated him so much, wouldn't they be angry if he stole some to eat? As he hesitated the birds came back, this time squawking loudly, then returned to their perches. Did they mean him to follow? Quickly he stood up, grabbed the basket and ran towards the cliff. Above his head he saw small crevices in the rock face. Some birds sat on what was, obviously, their nests, but a few ledges were empty. Finding openings he climbed with sure-footed confidence until he was looking straight into a nest holding several eggs. The birds twittered softly. Feeling rather foolish he cried out,

'I'm sorry to take your eggs, but I'm so very, very hungry and there is nothing else for me to eat here. I'm sure you'll be able to lay others quite soon,' and without waiting he hastily picked them up one by one and put them into the basket, carefully climbing down again so as not to break any. But there were no reprisals from the birds. It seemed they were willing him to take their eggs.

Raw eggs were not his favourite food but there was no choice and sitting down on the sand, he gently broke them one by one. Two had tiny embryos of fledglings but the rest appeared to be new laid and putting his head back let their soft, slimy contents slide over his tongue and into his gullet. Ah! He felt better, but now longed for something to drink. Once again, as if his thoughts were being listened to, he heard the sound of running water coming from a crevice in the rocks high above him. From a trickle it grew to a steady waterfall then made its way to the river across the sandy cove. It had not been there before, but Chato cared not, merely ran towards it and cupping his hands filled them with the refreshing, cool liquid, and drank deeply. Then he stood under the fall and let it soak his tired, bruised body until he felt cleansed and refreshed. The sudden coldness made him shiver, but he ran around the cove several times until the warmth came back. By this time he was naked and as he sat down again, he knew he had to cover himself with something before he tried to sleep. He picked up the blanket which was still damp. It would have to do. He threw it over his shoulders, drawing it tightly around him, and lay down beside his spear. His mind was so full of all that had happened to him that day, it was some time before he fell asleep. But before he slipped into unconsciousness he was aware that his body was warm and the blanket dry and comfortable.

The beginning of a new day and Chato woke to the sound of the river roaring and hurrying over the rocks once more. The sky was a deep blue but there was, as yet, little warmth from the sun. Immediately he remembered everything that had happened and looked round. There was no waterfall, no birds nesting on the cliffs; in fact no birds to be seen at all. Had it been his imagination? He stood up and walked to the river's edge. His canoe was still wedged between the rocks and now he could see clearly that it had a very large hole in the bottom. It could never be used again.

The damaged canoe was the least of his worries. How to get out of this cove and continue his journey with no boat seemed an impossible task. But first he had to find food to give him strength. He daren't gather eggs again for fear of angering the birds, but maybe he could catch a fish. Picking up his spear he walked over to the river's edge and gazed into the foaming water. Yes, he could see salmon trying desperately to swim up-river and one came close enough for him to lean over and quickly thrust the spear into its flailing body. He stepped back quickly, holding the spear high. Now he could make fire, and with the flint rocks and the blanket which he tore into short pieces with the sharp point of the spear, flames soon rose, and he placed the fish on top. It did not take long for it to cook and soon he was wolfing the flesh down, spitting out the bones. He kept fuelling the fire with pieces of the blanket until the flames were high enough to hold the wet clothes from the basket over them until they were dry once more. Then he put every item on and suddenly he felt a confidence surging through him. He had survived this ordeal and was determined to carry on, no matter what perils might face him on the journey.

He walked to the outer edge of the cove and looked round in the direction of the river's course. It was still surging on at a tremendous speed, but he noticed the shingled cove where he was, continued in a narrow ledge, the cliff towering above and the sandy shingle disappearing into the river. He could make his way along this ledge; it was his only chance to find a way out of his present position. Turning back he picked up his bow, inserted the spear into the quiver beside the arrows carefully and threw them over his shoulder. The basket, now empty except for the precious flint stones, he put over his other arm then treading over the stones and sand, he edged his body round the side of the cove and stepped on to the narrow strip which seemed to carry for some distance on while the rushing waters passed by. He had to hold on tightly to the cliff, searching for crevices and holes in the rocks, but slowly, and a trifle fearfully, he made his way towards a destiny that even yet he had no idea of its consequences.

CHAPTER 9

As he made his way along the ledge, desperately but carefully feeling for cracks and crevices in the rocks with his fingers and, without looking down, sliding one bare foot after the other to keep his balance, Chato was finding it difficult to think ahead to any ending of his journey. The river raced by only a short distance from his heels; the spray had already soaked him and once more his clothes were wet. Fear gripped him but strangely it gave him courage. He knew he was fighting for his life. One false step and he'd be dragged into the teeming waters. He doubted if this time he'd survive. All he could see in front of his face was hard, black rock and the noise behind deafened any cries for help to whatever spirit might be listening to him.

Slowly, slowly. His fingers became cold, the tips bleeding from contact with the sharp rock-face, but still he clung on, determined to come through this trial. And then, amazingly, the cliff was becoming shorter. He looked up, and could see more of the sky. He looked ahead and there was an ending as if some giant fork of lightning had split the rocks asunder and thrown them into the waters. His heart lifted, but still cautious, he made his way along the ledge which by this time had broadened, and soon he was standing on firmer ground. Not a cove this time, but a sparse rocky plain which stretched far into the distance where he could just make out the beginnings of a forest. The river had come through the ravine and now, exhausted went on its way calmly and deliberately to its ultimate fate.

Chato ran as far away from it as he could and threw himself down on the ground. He'd triumphed! At least for the moment.

Once again his immediate task was to find food and make fire. More important than the wet clothes. Taking off as much as was necessary, and placing them on the ground he first went back to the river to see if he could catch a fish. There were all kinds, swimming lazily now that the waters had ceased their turbulence and it was easy to spear them. Soon he had filled the basket with whitefish, a huge pike and some smaller fish, enough to last him for some time. As he turned, his foot struck what he thought was a stone under the shallow waters. He bent down and scooped it up. A large clam. 'What a find,' he thought. He gathered as many as he could. He would have a better meal than the previous night, that was sure, and the next day he'd go hunting for bigger prey.

By the time fire had been made, the food cooked and eaten and clothes dried off, Chato's feeling of well-being and confidence had returned. He *was* a brave. No matter what trials were put in his way he knew he'd overcome them all. And weren't the Spirits guiding him?

Wrapped up in his now dry clothes he lay down, the clear night sky above him and the distant noises of wolves and other animals creating a kind of lullaby that soon lulled him to sleep.

At the sun's rise Chato awoke slowly, remembered where he was and stretched his young body. He was all eagerness to travel on, for this was now becoming a wonderful adventure. But in what direction? Follow the river or go further into the plains? He'd make no decision until he was washed and had eaten the remainder of the fish cooked the previous night. And so, clothed in his leggings and leather tunic, arrows and spear over one shoulder, the basket over the other, he eventually set off across the rocky ground, towards the distant trees. His first thought was to kill some animal for meat and his eyes darted this way and that. He preferred small game, meat that could be cooked and eaten in one day, such as squirrels or wood rats. He made his way between the rocks and boulders, listening, searching. At first there was nothing. Then from behind a rock darted a beaver, trying to scamper back to the river. With lightning speed, Chato dropped the basket, had his bow and an arrow in his hands, and aiming, brought it down quickly and cleanly. One down; how many more? Within a short space of time, the basket held two wood rats, two beavers, a muskrat and several handfuls of blackberries which he'd found on a bush behind a large boulder. So early and yet so profitable! Chato grew greedy. Was there something bigger out there? A coyote, perhaps? He walked on, stealthily, hardly realising he was approaching the trees. Suddenly there was a loud squealing and from out the woods ran two bear cubs, closely followed by a grey-skinned cougar. It lunged forward and grabbed one by its throat, pulling it to the ground and sinking its fangs into the flesh. The other ran towards Chato, who drew his arrow to kill it; but suddenly the air was filled with the birds again. Eagles. For Chato time seemed to stand still as, with his bow pulled back and the arrow still in its groove, he looked at it. The shivering youngster's eyes were large, pleading.

Don't kill me! they said.

The moment passed and Chato let his arm fall. The eagles were still hovering above him, and it seemed they were trying to warn him. He had been told by Red Cloud to avoid contact with bears, any bears, and these were no different. How could he kill youngsters? Then he glanced at the cougar which by this time had put an end to the other cub's life and was tearing at the flesh and devouring it hungrily, completely unaware of Chato's presence. Unaware, too, of a new noise coming from the woods; a roaring, howling cry of rage. Just as Chato lifted his arrow once more and aimed at the cougar, the mother bear bounded out. The arrow found its mark and before the bear reached its offspring, the cougar was dead, its teeth still gripping the throat of the cub. Up above the birds squawked, dipping and diving. The bear stopped, seemed to be listening to them, then slowly went towards its dead cub and muzzled it. But it was no use. The mother made soft grunts, then turned to Chato. Her other cub stood beside him, unharmed. It seemed she took in the scene at a glance, looked up at the birds and then to Chato's amazement, spoke.

It seems you are not my enemy. I have you to thank for saving at least one of my youngsters. The birds have told me of your journey through these parts. Because of your action I shall send word to all my family that you are not to be harmed as you travel. But you too must promise not to harm any of us.

The birds seemed to hover motionless as if waiting for Chato's answer. His mind could hardly grasp that once again the birds had come to his aid. This in spite of his killing one of them. And the bear had spoken, just as the Spirit of the Wind and the birds themselves had done too. There was some unnatural force at work here, but he was not going to question it for the present. Instead he said,

'Certainly I shall not harm your family. You must take my word for that as I do yours. Now may I ask a favour from you? What is the best way to travel towards the river's end? Should I go through the plains or follow the river itself? I am alone and need to hunt for my food.'

The bear thought for a moment.

Your best plan would be to keep to the plains, but parallel to the river. You will eventually come to a village where you will, I'm sure be given shelter.

At these words the eagles began to screech, flying up and down in a frenzy, and as quickly as they had arrived, flew off again. The bear looked up then shook her head. There were no more words to come from her mouth, but gently nudging her remaining cub back towards the woods, she turned to look at Chato and pointed her snout in the direction of the river's course, but well clear of its water's edge. In an instant she was gone. Once more the young brave could hardly believe what had happened, but there was the carcase of the bear and the dead cougar to prove it. What should he do with them? Their meat would be too heavy to carry on his journey but if left like that they'd be at the mercy of the carrion crows and buzzards. He thought of the bear he'd spared, now without its young sibling to play with and remembered his own brothers and sister who must be missing him at the moment. No, he couldn't leave them like this. He had no tool to dig a grave but there must be branches and twigs in the woods, he thought, to cover them completely. He knew his friends back in the village would be roaring with laughter if they could see him now, but somehow their opinion wasn't important anymore.

Once the bodies had been covered over, he took up his weapons and belongings and set forward in the direction the mother bear had indicated. It would be interesting to reach this village. Just to be with people again would be worth everything that had happened to him since he set out on Red Cloud's canoe. He squared his shoulders, confidence growing with every step.

CHAPTER 10

The plain stretched far ahead of him as did the river, lazy now after its ferocious passage through the ravine. Chato felt secure and hopeful. There would be fish aplenty and small animals to hunt amongst the trees. By the time he reached this village that the bear had talked about, he'd be in good shape. Would the tribe be friendly? He had had no experience of any other peoples outside his own village and only from the stories that the older tribesmen told around the fires at night did he learn that there were any other tribes in the world around them. He began to feel quite excited.

For the rest of that day he filled his basket with fish, some river mussels and shellfish. He even brought down a waterfowl and when he ventured into the woods, came across a turkey which was so surprised to be disturbed that it had no time to flee from Chato's arrow. He began to feel quite proud of his archery skills and only wished Red Cloud was here to see how well he'd progressed. He did lament the loss of the corn-cakes and vegetables tipped into the river when the canoe capsized. Still, there were nuts and berries to be picked in the woods, he was sure.

Several days went by and still he hadn't come across the village. He noticed that the river was widening, that it was sending out small streams on either side, and he could now spear fish from these pools without going near the river itself. And he suddenly became aware of a strange smell and a fresh breeze. He sniffed. It wasn't a river smell; that was for sure. The ground began to rise and he was climbing steeply. At the top of the hill he stopped, astonished at what he saw. The plains that he had carefully and sometimes painfully walked over were coming to an end and there in front of him was nothing but water. The river too was emptying its contents into this vast space. He was confused. Where was he to go? Was this the end of his journey? Suddenly he felt cheated. To turn back at this stage with no great trophy to show for his troubles would be humiliating. He looked over at the forest. What a fool he'd been; too busy catching food to keep alive, he'd forgotten the real reason for this journey. To show his bravery and that meant catching a wild animal worthy of his skill. Turning his back on the distant water he walked back down the hill and crossed over to the trees. He was going to stalk the biggest animal he could find----except a bear of course.

Cautiously he approached, his spear held high, eyes darting this way and that. As he made his way through the undergrowth, the trees above him, in full leaf, gradually blotted out the sun and he had to peer intently to see anything at all. Was that an elk, a wapiti, staring at him from behind that cedar? He raised his spear, but just as he was about to aim, there was a rattling sound and a large snake uncoiled itself a short distance from his feet. In terror he dropped his weapon. The elk took flight, and Chato, desperately trying to take an arrow from his quiver, slipped on the mossy ground and landed close to the snake which raised its head, hissed loudly and with darting tongue closed its fangs on Chato's ankle. The sudden attack and the pain of the bite into his flesh made him cry out, 'Ahhhhhhhh!' He stood up, stepped back and tried again to pull out an arrow, but the snake hissed and waved its round flat head from side to side, its malevolent eyes firmly fixed on Chato's own. This hypnotic stare seemed to paralyse the boy. His mind raced, trying to think of a way out of this situation, but he could think of nothing. The snake was in his way and seemed determined to keep him here. He looked at his ankle where there was now a round, jagged tear in the skin and blood seeping through. The snake still looked dangerous, so he began to move backwards, slowly at first, then faster in his anxiety to put as much distance between it and himself as possible. But suddenly there was a numbness in his foot, then in his legs. He stumbled, fell and struck his head against a broad tree trunk. There was a ringing sound in his ears, his eyes glazed over and he lost consciousness.

The forest was silent. Then from afar a solitary eagle soared towards the immobile boy. It swooped and landed beside him, walking around, observing, then just as swiftly took off again.

The boy's body lay there for some time and the silence was almost tangible. Not a bird, not an animal made a sound. They were there but either in respect or perhaps in awe, they remained hidden.

Then, through the trees, from the other side, came voices.

'Do you see him yet? We must get to him as quickly as possible. If we don't treat him soon he'll die.

One by one a group of men approached the figure lying on the ground. The first to reach him knelt down and looked him over critically. Their voices had

penetrated Chato's mind and barely conscious, eyes glazed, he tried to say, 'Please help me,' but all that came out of his open mouth was a gurgle. A second man muttered,

'There is the snake wound, on his ankle.'

He lifted up the boy's foot and placing his teeth over the open tear he bit out a piece of flesh and turning his head spat it out. A second man gave him a large leaf on which was spread a soft gluey substance, and this was wrapped round the ankle completely covering the wound. More leaves were used to seal it. During all this time Chato appeared dazed, but he was sufficiently conscious to realise that these men spoke words he could understand, but the sounds were broader, harsher. He struggled to get to his feet, but was held down by the first man.

'No, no, young man. Don't move. We shall carry you back to our tribe where you'll be looked after. Anyway you'll soon feel sleepy and sleep is what you need.'

Chato was picked up by two others and slowly the group departed the way they had entered, back through the forest and out the other side to a large open space where their village was. But not like the one Chato came from. Here, instead of tepees, there were several huge longhouses with sloping roofs, made from planks of cedar wood. The first man, obviously the leader said to the others,

'We'll take him to my house where the women will care for him now. I think we rescued him in time.'

As they carried Chato to the entrance, he came to complete consciousness and looked around at the men who had carried him all this way. What he saw was a sight he could not have imagined even in his wildest dreams. Were they men? Or birds? They walked like men, had arms and legs like men, but all over their bodies sprouted feathers. They wore little clothing and he could see that on their backs the feathers were thick and long, almost like wings. He looked up at the sky. No birds to be seen. And yet how did the men know he had been bitten by the snake? There was more mystery here. At every occasion when he'd needed help some spirit seemed to come to his rescue.

Inside the longhouse two women came towards him, twittering and clucking as they saw how distressed Chato was.

'The poor boy! Leave him to us. We'll dress the snake wound every day until it heals. And the right foods will help him recover.'

Chato saw kindliness in their faces, but as the snake's poison worked its way through his body and before he slipped back into unconsciousness, they became blurred and then one, as he imagined it was his mother who looked at him.

CHAPTER 11

Chato's recovery was slow, for when the next day began, after a fretful sleep he awoke, feverish and twitching, calling out words that were rambling, unconnected and making no sense to the women tending to him. They took off the makeshift dressing from his wound, cleaned it then applied a different substance, this time a green paste that made Chato gag at the horrible smell and give a scream as it stung his flesh. He tried to sit up and push their hands away, but he had no strength. Panic rose within him. Was he dying? Were they poisoning him?

'There now,' said one. 'Don't fret. We shall not harm you. Just sleep and the poison will disappear.'

Chato thrashed about on the blanket. He had a fear of these strange people but he was helpless, in their thrall.

The woman looked at his shaking body.

'Poor child. The poison is affecting him and it will be some time before our herbs cast it out. We must just wait.'

She gently stroked his brow as another woman wrapped a soft bandage of hemp cloth around his ankle. Gradually the stinging sensation disappeared and Chato slowly drifted into a more settled sleep. He was unaware when three men entered the longhouse. Two went immediately to separate groups of women and children, their families, housed in their own sections of the house. The third, who was the leader, stopped at Chato's mat and knelt down beside the women. The one who had spoken looked at him.

'Where did you find this boy, Paco? Do you know where he comes from, what tribe he belongs to?'

'I don't know,' her man replied angrily. 'We didn't really find him. It was the eagle that told us where he was and to bring him here.'

'The eagle?' Her voice quivered. 'But we haven't done anything wrong or wicked for a very long time.'

'No, but this boy has committed the sin of killing one of his flock and he has taken his revenge by leading him to us. You know what that means, don't you?'

His woman, Tadi, took in a swift breath as she heard these words. Of course she knew. This young brave would never go back to his home, would never see his family or friends. Instead he'd be initiated into their culture, the culture of the eagle people. The whole process would begin again. She looked at the sleeping Chato. Such a handsome youth. Just like another son. How would he react when he came to his full senses, to be told what was about to happen?

The next day Chato awoke, his mind clearer and his eyes more focused. It all seemed like a dream, but as he looked around at the numbers of people lying or sitting in this building, he knew that it wasn't. They seemed to be in groups, and his group included a woman whom he recognised as one who had tended to him, a man whose face was turned away, and several others whose bodies were covered in blankets that it was unclear whether they were men or women. He stretched his arms, then his legs which had lost that numb feeling, and tried to rise from the blanket, but the movements woke the man who turned then jumped up to push Chato back down. It was Paco.

'No, my young brave. Stay where you are. Your strength has not returned yet. Let us help. We shall not harm you, I promise.'

He began to gently caress Chato's face. This was going to be a slow process, but with gentleness it could be done. His drew his fingers slowly down the boy's cheeks, then his throat and bare chest. Chato noticed the small, short feathers covering the back of the man's hands and now in the light coming through the open door it was evident that he had short feathers all over him. Not thickly, but as if human hair had been replaced by a feathery growth. The boy shivered and he felt a tingling on his skin. He looked down at his body, but it seemed to be the same as before. Perhaps this was just part of their skills to heal him from the snake's bite. Paco continued like this for some time then, stopping, said over his shoulder,

'Get up, Tadi. We all need to eat, especially this young man.'

All the women rose as if one and proceeded to cook. They produced a meal that Chato had never tasted before; strange fish from the sea and a large shellfish that he later learned was called a lobster. Meat from the huge bison and other large animals. What astonished him were the eyes of these creatures, boiled in the women's cooking pots and put before him. He shrank back at the idea of eating them, but the women were insistent. Instead of speaking, they indicated that the food was good for him, by tasting some themselves and rubbing their stomachs and rolling their eyes in delight. They laughed as he tried to swallow what to him was an obscenity, but to his surprise the taste was not as vile as he'd supposed.

That day he was fed, his wound attended to, and at one point a young girl, rather lovely but with soft feathers sprouting from her arms and legs beneath her tunic of deer skin, approached him. Shyly, she began to speak, her voice soft, with a tuneful rise and fall to its cadences.

'I am Tansi, daughter of Chief Paco. What is your name? Are you better?'

Chato swallowed and in a rather croaking voice said,

'I thank you, Tansi. My name is Chato, and yes, I do feel a little stronger. But I'm still confused as to where I am.'

The woman called Tadi came over to them. She pointed at the girl.

'Tansi, my daughter, will be your companion until you are fit to go hunting with the men. The other women and I will make sure your wound is completely healed before then.'

Tansi smiled and the smile lit up her face. If it wasn't for the feathers she'd be just as pretty as Natane, he thought. A sudden pang gripped him. How he longed to be back with his own tribe. Would they all forget him? Would Natane find another brave to be her man? The very thought made him miserable and a scowl came over his boyish face. Tansi's smile disappeared when she saw this.

'Are you in pain?' she asked.

He shook his head and turned away from her, leaving her hurt and her mother upset. But he did not see their faces and suddenly did not care. This "punishment adventure" was not turning out as he had thought.

There was another session with the leader, Paco, stroking his body from head to toes with his fingers, and much more of the delicious food that the women were determined he should eat. By the time nightfall came Chato was ready to close his eyes and fall into a deep sleep.

He woke early. The thin light of morning came through the open entrance. Everyone else was still asleep. He stretched as he did before and in the light saw his arms. They were covered in a feathery down. He drew the cover away from his body. His legs were the same and already the down was sprouting from his chest. His heart began to beat wildly. Panic brought a tightening of his throat and he tried to scream out, but there was no sound. What had happened to him? What had that man done? He was turning into an eagle man. The tears welled up in his eyes and suddenly, like the river dashing through the ravine they overflowed and he sobbed uncontrollably. The noise wakened Paco and Tadi. They rose quickly and went over.

'Hush, hush,' whispered the woman. 'You'll disturb the children.'

She looked at Paco then back at the boy. She touched him, feeling the soft downy feathers on his naked body.

'It's happening so soon! It took longer with us, did it not?'

'Yes, but we were the first. Perhaps the eagle has plans for this boy and has increased my powers. Anyway we are in no position to question its reasons. We do what we have to do.'

He knelt down to comfort Chato who shrank back in terror. Paco took the boy's face in his hands, making him look into his eyes and gradually the sobs gave way to nervous gulps as he sucked in air. The man stood up and pulled Chato to his feet. At first he swayed and would have fallen if Paco hadn't kept a tight hold of him.

'Woman,' he said to Tadi. 'Give this boy something to cover his nakedness.'

She brought a short tunic and pulled it over Chato's head. Gently Paco led him out of the longhouse into the pale morning sunshine where he was made to sit, cross-legged, on the soft earth, in front of the opening. Kneeling beside him, Paco began,

'You are frightened at what is happening to your body. You are becoming like us so before any more time goes by I have to tell you about the eagle and what we have suffered.'

As his words penetrated Chato's mind, the impact of them filled his heart with horror.

CHAPTER 12

There was a bundle of long, thin tree branches propped against the wall and Paco had pulled out one of them to help emphasise his story. Before beginning he drew with the point of the stick the outline of an eagle on the soft earth. Feverishly he filled it in and slowly the image of a vicious bird took shape. An angry face, feathers flying and wings outstretched as if in flight.

'This is the Master. This is the creature that has placed such a punishment upon us. And it was not such a terrible crime. We killed animals every day in order to survive and the older braves taught the young ones their skills in using their weapons, especially the bow and arrow. We were a happy tribe, until one day a boy about as old as you, stupidly set off an arrow and it brought down an eagle,'---

'Just as I did!' interrupted Chato. 'But I didn't mean to kill it.'

Paco nodded his head.

'It made no difference to the eagle. Suddenly it appeared above us, an enormous bird. So large that its outspread wings blotted out the sun and everything was dark. Behind   flew many smaller eagles. They swooped down upon us, pecking at our heads and faces. We were terrified. Our women and children cowered down and set up an enormous wailing, such as I'd never heard before. Then the Master, to my astonishment spoke directly to me. It said,

> *You are the leader of these people so I say these words to you. A terrible crime has been committed against us, the great eagles of the air. You must pay the penalty. As from now you will be half man/ half bird, and will give allegiance to ME and my flock. You will be feathered, but your wings will not be strong enough to fly and if any of you try to escape this place by any other means they will be killed immediately. Also, if another of our eagles is brought down we shall kill every one of you. I shall know all that you do and even what you think and can be in contact at any time. Meanwhile you will continue your lives as normal, but beware of my wrath!*

With these words' continued Paco, 'it flapped its enormous wings and flew off, the others following.   My family and the rest of the tribe remained in shock for quite some time, but gradually we began to speak amongst ourselves, saying,

'This can't be true.'

'The Spirits have put a spell upon us and we have been dreaming'

Tadi, my woman, said,

'Of course we've been dreaming. An eagle couldn't possibly speak to us.'

'Believing this we all went about our duties as before, until a few days later I woke to discover I was covered in downy feathers. You who have experienced this too, can understand my terror. And that terror engulfed the whole tribe. It was a very difficult time adjusting to the change in us, and many of the braves refused to go hunting for fear of being attacked again. But I gathered a council and we sat down together to plan how we were to live under these circumstances. We decided that life had to go on as usual and so it has. What you see around you is a tribe of eagle people, but with hearts of men. Do you understand?'

Chato nodded but deep down there was a question he felt he must ask.

'Did any of your braves try to escape?'

'Oh yes. But their horribly mutilated bodies were dropped from the skies by the Master's killer birds. It was a lesson we never forgot.'

Chato thought again.

'And your wings, did none of you try them out?'

Paco stood up and turned his back which like the rest of him had a covering of feathers. To the boy's astonishment these feathers became firm and before his eyes thick feathery wings appeared. The eagle man flapped them as if about to fly but he remained on the ground. He shrugged his shoulders as if to say, *it's no good!*

The most important question for Chato to be answered was,

'Paco, how did you know where to find me?'

'The eagles fly over our village every day then I suppose they fly back to the Master and report on us. But one day it was the master

77

eagle itself that came to tell us about *your* crime and that you were to be punished as we were. We were directed to you and we brought you back here. The rest you know. But what I've not told you yet is that I was given the powers to transform you, something I'd never attempted before. I was astonished at how well I did it!'

Chato did not echo that astonishment. Misery overwhelmed him. He'd never see his village again. Never see Natane or be able to take her as his woman. Oh, that he had died. Better to have no life than live half-man, half-bird. Sending him down the river had been the Chief's and Red Cloud's idea to give him a chance to redeem himself; prove he really was a brave. But the eagle had had other plans and everything that had happened since the beginning of his journey was predestined by this so-called Master.

Paco saw the boy's sad face. He stood up, and helped Chato to his feet.

'It won't be so bad, you'll see. Other than our feathers we live a good life.'

They returned to the interior of the longhouse where already the morning meal was ready. Tadi saw them and came over. She looked anxiously at Paco.

'Have you managed to tell him yet? It must have been a great shock.'

'Yes, it was, but I believe he understands our position now and accepts his.'

Tadi nodded, looking at Chato. They would have to be gentle with him. Already she felt as if he was her son.

And so Chato's new life took shape. Day followed day, the moon grew and died and grew again as it always did, and slowly he was initiated into the ways of the eagle people. Tansi became his companion, showing him round the village where he met other braves and young girls. Apart from their feathery bodies they did not look too different from his friends back home and as his strength returned he was gradually accepted into their world. To them he was now an eagle man. At least Tansi thought so. She kept by his side, laughing up into his face as if to say to the other girls, *he is going to be my man!* But Chato kept his distance. He laughed with them all, showed off his skills with the bow and arrow, but always there was that one thought. He *must* try to return to his tribe.

Came the day when Paco decided he was strong enough to go hunting. The forest around the village teemed with wild life and every day the hunters returned with enough meat and fish to feed their families to excess. Chato had never eaten so well. But the greatest surprise was when they led him to the end of the river and he looked out upon the expanse of water that he had seen from the hilltop. Paco noticed his astonishment.

'This is the mighty river that never ends,' he said. 'In the past, before our disgrace, some of our men built canoes and set off to discover where this water goes, but they never returned. We think they may have slipped over the edge out there.'

He pointed into the distance.

'Since we've become eagle people no one has dared try again. But we gather the shellfish in the shallows and occasionally catch a turtle. It's best not to travel too far away for fear of angering the Master.'

Chato was about to say, 'Couldn't you have tried just once' but remained silent. Suddenly he realised that although he had become as them, an eagle man, and had grown feathers instead of hairs, deep down he was still the same Chato. His thoughts were not their thoughts. He still longed for his village, for his family, but how could he get back to them? It seemed impossible. He looked up at the sky where birds of all kinds were flying freely, some of them eagles that came down close as if to spy on the men. He looked at their wings. Of course, that was it. Paco had shown him that the feathers on their backs were really wings. These people were so scared of the eagle they would do nothing to help themselves. But he was different. He was from a different tribe, a tribe of true braves, and if he was developing wings on his shoulders, then he would make them strong, strong enough to carry him home.

That night as he sat outside the longhouse, the sun casting a copper glow as it ended its progress across the sky, he began to make his plans. He knew his body was strong now, but the next task was to flex his shoulder muscles and produce powerful wings. Then, in secret, flap them to see if he could rise from the ground. And when he was ready he'd leave this place and fly back to his own people. His spirits rose--- but were dashed when from inside he heard Tadi's voice.

'Our Tansi seems very taken with Chato. It would be a very good thing if he took her as his woman. Don't you think so, Paco ?'

'Yes. He would bring new blood into our family and he's very strong. I'll speak to her, for I'm sure she'll want this. I've never seen her so happy in any young man's company before.'

Chato froze where he sat. He was being trapped, slowly but surely. Tansi was more like a sister to him, whereas the one girl he wanted, Natane, was back in his village. He became angry and without thinking got up and entered the house. Paco and Tadi looked startled on seeing him so upset.

'What's the matter, Chato?' asked Tadi.

'I heard what you said about Tansi and me. I do NOT want to take her.

His voice tembled and he was almost in tears.

'There is a girl in my village waiting for me and I'm going to fly back there. I don't want to spend the rest of my life here with you.'

His voice grew louder and he shook with rage. Paco and Tadi stood as statues, looks of horror on their faces. What was he saying? Then Paco, trying to calm him, said,

'You cannot do this. You've been brought here as punishment and the eagle would never allow you to escape. Please think carefully. Anyway the wings you have are not strong enough for flying.'

'I shall make them strong and then I'll leave this place!'

Tadi began to weep and some of the other women who had heard Chato's words, joined in, their wailing a concerted sound of despair. Paco looked solemn and, turning, he went to the centre of the longhouse and clapped his hands loudly. All the men came from their little groups and gathered round him. They sat down, huddled together, listening as Paco talked and now and again making their own suggestions. Chato slowly calmed down and was regretting his outburst. It seemed a long time before Paco arose and came towards the boy.

'We have discussed what you say you'll do, but are sure that the Master, who knows everything, would not allow you to escape and return to your village. However we have come to a solution. It's obvious your people will no longer accept you as an eagle man but if you wish this girl to be your woman then you should fly to her and bring her back here. I'm sure you'd both be happy, especially when she is made an eagle too. But the Master will have to be told exactly why we have taken this decision and you can be sure your journey will be spied upon.'

Chato thought deeply. It seemed a possibility. At least he didn't have to live with Tansi. The thought that his own tribe would not welcome him now had not occurred to him and he suddenly felt lost. He could learn to fly and go and fetch Natane, but would she come with him? It was a risk he had to take. If he did not bring her back what kind of life would he have? He nodded at Paco.

'I'll do that. When I've grown my wings I'll leave here and return before the white rain falls.'

The men's troubled faces broke into smiles and they turned back to their work. Paco went over to Tadi and whispered in her ear. Her brown eyes grew large. She looked at Tansi, who was standing alongside her, dejected, Chato's words so unexpected and harsh. Her mother gave a sigh.

'I'm sorry for our daughter. She had set her heart on being taken by Chato. But at least this decision will not bring the eagle's wrath down upon us all. Still, I'm disappointed.'

'Our feelings are not important,' said Paco. 'We live in constant fear of our master and we must never, never cross him. We must just hope that it will all work out.'

And so life in the longhouse returned to normal. Chato went hunting every day, but always he flexed his shoulder muscles, and kept looking over them to see how his wings were growing. And grow they did, until one morning he spread them out and flapped them. To his delight they took on a steady rhythm, and his feet left the ground. Only a little way, but it was a beginning. He began to make his plans.

CHAPTER 13

Chato's attempts at strengthening his shoulders and flapping his rather weak, puny wings had the other boys and girls giggling and making rude remarks.

'Think you'll take off, Chato?' one asked, rolling his eyes and making flying movements with his arms. They had all roared with laughter. Until the day he was suddenly seen hovering above them, his now strong wings outstretched. No laughter now; only amazement. Not one person in the tribe had had the thinking power or the courage to imagine they could have tried the same thing. The eagle had sealed their fate and that was the end of it. Their life was still the same as long as they didn't leave the village. But now here was someone who challenged that fate in spite of the dangers. A surge of excitement raced through them.

'You've done it, Chato! But how? Can you show us?' asked one of the previous doubters. Chato slowly flew down and landed beside them. Before he tucked the wings in to his body, they could see how long, sinewy and strong they were. So different to the small weak apologies behind their backs.

'I worked hard, day after day,' said Chato, 'for I was determined. Your teasing only made me more sure that I was doing the right thing, for really your opinion means nothing. Yes, I could show you what to do, but it will have to wait. I'm leaving here very soon and flying back to my village where I hope to persuade the only girl I want, to return with me.'

'But the Master!' shouted a girl from the back of the group. 'It will be so angry.'

'Are you all so afraid of it? The eagles are only birds and I'm sure if you all fought back you could destroy them.'

They stood looking at him and some of them shook their heads.

'Some of us have tried, but they were killed. We're not strong enough to bring it and all the flock down.' This was said by one of the older boys.

Chato shrugged his shoulders. He was not really interested.

'I shall leave, no matter what you say,' and he walked back to the longhouse where Paco and Tadi were waiting for him. They had seen him taking his first flight and guessed he was ready to go. The sun had already risen.

'I hope you realise there is great danger in what you're about to do.' Paco showed his concern.

'I've been through so much peril since I left home that I'm sure I'll overcome anything the eagle does to bring me down.'

Once again Chato's pride and arrogance appeared. He felt strong now that he knew his wings were capable of carrying him and all he could think of was what his people would think when they saw him.

Tadi had made him a tunic with openings in the back for his wings to be pushed through, and filled a small basket with dried meat and berries. When he was ready, he slung this, together with his beloved bow and quiver of new arrows through a rope of plaited hemp and tied it securely around his waist. He looked at Paco.

'I leave you now. Thank you for rescuing me. Hopefully we shall see each other again, but if anything happens to me before I return, know that I shall always be grateful for your goodness.'

Tadi had tears in her eyes and Paco, much as he'd have liked to put his arms around Chato in farewell, merely stood back and said,

'May the Spirits go with you.'

The boy turned away and walked confidently out of the longhouse, taking long strides which became a run. He slowly flapped his wings; they developed a steady rhythm and with one great lunge he was in the air and flying above them. Others had come to watch and they gazed, mesmerised at the sight.

'It can't be possible!' said one woman.

'It certainly is!' said another.

The object of their fascination flew higher and in the direction of the river. That river he'd navigated so recently. But this time he would be following it back to his village. Chato's excitement grew. His wings were strong; he could feel their strength as they beat regularly behind him.

He looked down at the water and it was hard to believe the journey he'd made. Now he could see its expanse, stretching ahead in the distance towards the mountains. He was seeing it all as the birds did. Could see beyond the bends, the high rocks. What freedom! He was so elated that he did not at first realise the sky was growing darker, the sun no longer shining down. He looked up thinking to see clouds covering it, but no; the birds had followed him and were blocking out the light. They screeched and croaked, swooping down to his level as if to attack, but never touching. It put him off balance and his wings faltered. He dropped, but with as much effort as he could muster, he flapped and flapped until once more he was steady and flying evenly. The birds turned and disappeared as quickly as they had come, uncovering the sun which shone out of its blue sky again. Chato's heart beat wildly for a time then settled into a rhythm to match his wings. His determination and courage grew.

This journey up river was faster and safer; past the ravine and the rapids which had all but ended his life. He followed the turns and bends, where the dead birds had floated to the surface, and then he saw the rows of tepees that he knew so well. He began to descend. There was the totem pole outside the Chief's tent. And there was Red Cloud's. His wings slowed their beating, and he landed. He looked round. Where was everybody? There should be children playing, women working outside. Instead there was a deathly silence. He walked to the Chief's tepee and put his head inside. It was empty. No fire, no smell of cooking. He went over to the tent he knew so well, Red Cloud's.

It was the same. Frantically he ran to find his parents, but they were nowhere. He ran here and there, calling names of friends, family, and finally arrived at Natane's tent, where he found her lying on a blanket, alone and weak. He knelt down.

'Natane!' he cried. 'It's me, Chato. I've come back. But where is everyone?'

She looked at him with blank eyes then tried to sit up.

'Ch-ch-chato? Is it you? I thank the Spirits that you've come to save us, or what's left of us.'

'What's left of you? Tell me what has happened.'

She sank back.

'After you went away the fish continued to die in the river. And there were no animals for our braves to hunt or capture. We had no food and what was in reserve the adults fed us, the young ones and starved themselves. Gradually they died, even my parents and yours. Now there is nothing and I'm just waiting to die too.'

Her eyes filled with tears.

Chato could hardly take this in, but then he put his hands round her shoulders and lifted her up so she sat close to his chest.

'You are not going to die. Things have happened to me since I left and I'm no longer the same Chato. Look carefully. Do you see the feathers? Can you feel them?'

She put out her hand and stroked his arm, touched his cheek where, instead of the first bloom of manly beard, there were small downy plumages. Her eyes widened.

'Yes, I'm like a bird,' and carefully he began telling her of his adventures and how he had been rescued by the eagle people. How they had angered a king eagle, or the Master, and had been turned into these creatures as punishment.

'Because I'd killed an eagle they were told by the bird to find me and transform me to be as them. But I'm not! I have feathers, yes, but I'm still Chato, a son of this tribe, and vowed to return home.'

He told her how he'd built up strong wings, and had flown all the way home to find out if she would still be his woman, and agree to go back to the other tribe with him. For there was no way the Master would let him stay here. Anyway he was now an eagle man and she could become one too.

Natane froze in his arms. His story was almost unbelievable. But there were the feathers to prove his words. She looked at her body, so thin, so pale. If Chato hadn't come she'd probably die in a few suns. She looked up at his face, that still handsome face that had always attracted her. What would it be like, this strange place of eagle people? Finding out would be better than dying.

'I think I should like to come with you, Chato, but am I strong enough?'

'I have the strength for both of us. Quickly now, before the night falls.' And he helped her out of the tepee. They were both surprised to see several of Chato's old friends gathered outside. They had heard the beating of his wings as he'd approached and were curious to see who or what it was.

'Chato! You've come back.' The voice was weak but he recognised Eskadi. Chato made no answer. He was too concerned with making sure the rope round his waist was firm and that his weapons were secure. He picked Natane up in his arms, began to run, flapping his wings and slowly he left the ground. He knew he was carrying a little more weight, but suddenly was surprised by a pulling at his ankle. Eskadi had grabbed it and was flying with him. Another boy grabbed *his* foot, and he in turn grabbed another's, and so it went on like this, girls too until the entire group were behind him, flying together in one long line. Chato felt himself falling, then with a mighty effort, flapped his wings strongly until their beat became steady again and he, Natane and the strange row of young braves and girls flew in a long line like a streamer of plaited grasses.

They hadn't gone far when, as if out of the sun, the Master eagle appeared above them. Its huge feathered wings spread over Chato and it dived and swooped trying to snatch Natane from his arms. The face was evil, the eyes red with anger and its talons extended to pull Chato's wings apart. Swiftly Chato dived too, out of its range, but two of his uninvited passengers were not so lucky. The last, they were plucked from their grip and torn to pieces. But in the time that the Master had devoured them then soared upwards, ready to swoop once more, Chato had a sudden thought. For the first time he was on a level with this bird, flying in his territory and he still had a weapon . His trusty arrows.

'Quick, Natane. Grab hold of the rope round my waist so that I can have both hands free.'

She did this and hung on tightly while he untied his bow and quiver. The wings were still beating strongly, and carefully he strung an arrow, turned his head towards the eagle as it dived and aiming quickly, shot it towards the bird but it flew past without striking. There was a screech, a great flapping of wings and Chato was almost put off balance as the mighty eagle swooped down upon him. But Chato had another weapon; a foot, the one that wasn't being held by the boy from his village. With frantic beatings of his wings and hoping that Natane was holding on with all her strength, he kicked out, this way and that, dodging the wicked talons and managing to strike with some force. The eagle flew up, ready to battle again, but now Chato had more time to take aim and his second shot was perfect. The arrow flew straight to the eagle's throat and the enormous bird stopped in mid-air. There was a deep croak, the wings collapsed and the creature fell heavily to the river below where its body was swiftly taken through the rapids, the force of the water breaking its body into a million pieces.

Chato's heart was hammering so loudly that there was a ringing in his ears. He'd done it! Killed the dreaded Monster. Now what would happen to all the eagle people? Surely they'd lose their fear now? And what about him and Natane? He looked down at her, still clinging to the rope. He slung his bow and quiver over his shoulder once more, unfastened her fingers and drew her up to his chest.

'Oh Natane, how brave you've been. But the Monster is dead and we have nothing to fear.'

He looked back and was astonished to see that the line of boys and girls was still streaming behind. He'd have to take them to the eagle people now. He wondered where all the other birds were and whether they'd be free too. He soon found out. Like a huge black cloud, they appeared, descended and flew round and round the group of flying youngsters. The noise they made was deafening and they certainly weren't friendly. But they did not attack and soon they formed together and left. Chato breathed a sigh of relief which did not last long. To his horror, the wings behind his back seemed to lose their regular beat. They stalled; he flapped them frantically but there was no response. He looked at his hands; there were no feathers. None on his legs and taking a quick look over his shoulder there were no wings! Which meant he couldn't fly! Already he was aware that they were losing height and soon they'd all fall into the river. Instinctively he called out,

'Oh Spirit of the Wind, help us. We've been through so much, we can't die now. Help us to land safely.'

At first there was no response and the river was rushing up to meet them. Then a soft sighing sound was heard.

The Spirit hears you, Chato. You have been the bravest of braves to kill the Monster of the skies and you and all your companions will be saved. But you will not return to the eagle people. You will fly, even without wings, to another land, another life. Now go!

Chato felt a rush of air underneath his body and once more he was flying. Natane nestled in his arms, exactly as before and the rest of the group were still holding on behind. He suddenly felt calm, but also a sense of pride. The Spirit had called him "the bravest of the brave." He'd achieved what he'd set out to do.

They flew over the river and then to the large water. Chato's fear returned. Where was the Spirit taking them? There was no place to land. Suddenly there was a mighty rumble and out of the water's depths arose islands. Rocks, trees, bushes appeared, and running about were animals of all kinds. Chato lost his fear as slowly they descended. The boys and girls let go their grip of each other's feet and two by two they landed on the islands. Chato and Natane found themselves on the largest one and looked around their new territory. For that's what it was. They knew they'd never return to their old tribe or village. Everything was gone. Here would be their home now.

****

And homes were made in all these islands. If you ever visit the western coast of northern Canada you may hear stories of Haida Gwaii, or the Queen Charlotte Islands. You may hear the Spirit of the Wind as it blows across the "river that never ends" echoing their names. *Cha-a-a-to, Nata-a-a-ne.*

Printed in the United Kingdom
by Lightning Source UK Ltd.
123303UK00002B/124-150/A

A long time ago the ancient peoples of North West Canada looked upon the eagle as a sacred bird. One day Chato, a young brave, disgraces himself and his tribe by shooting one down with his arrow. In revenge the Master eagle sends his flock to attack the villagers who, when they find out that Chato is the culprit want to kill him. But their chief, Eagle Eye, decides that he should be given the chance to prove he really is a brave and worthy of his place amongst the men in the village. So he is sent down river in a canoe, with only a spear and his beloved bow and arrows as weapons.

During the journey he experiences many hazards and adventures and each time he is saved by praying to the Spirits. Eventually he is rescued by the eagle people, so-called because of a spell put on them by the Master Eagle, and taken to their village. There they cast their own spell on him and he grows feathers. He still yearns for his own tribe and when he discovers the feathers on his back and undeveloped wings, he decides to make them strong, so that he can fly back to his village. He does this and begins the most thrilling adventure of ."

authorHOUSE®

ISBN 978-1-4343-2977-6

90000

9 781434 329776